This
Treasure Cove Story
belongs to

_____

_____

TROLLS WORLD TOUR

A CENTUM BOOK 978-1-913399-09-2
Published in Great Britain by Centum Books Ltd.
This edition published 2020.

1 3 5 7 9 10 8 6 4 2

Centum Books Ltd, 20 Devon Square, Newton Abbot,
Devon, TQ12 2HR, UK.

www.centumbooksltd.co.uk | books@centumbooksltd.co.uk
CENTUM BOOKS Limited Reg. No. 07641486.

A CIP catalogue record for this book is available
from the British Library.

Printed in China.

centum

A Treasure Cove Story

DreamWorks
Trolls
WORLD TOUR

By David Lewman

Illustrated by Priscilla Wong

It was a beautiful day in Trolls Village. Queen Poppy and the other Trolls were having fun singing, dancing and hugging, when Biggie arrived, calling, 'HELP! I'M BEING ATTACKED BY A MONSTER!'

The *monster* was just a bat with a message for Poppy. But who was it from?

Poppy read the message.
'Queen Barb? The Queen
of the Rocker Trolls?' she said.

King Peppy explained to Poppy that they were not
the only Trolls in the world. Poppy and her friends loved
pop music, so they were the Pop Trolls, but there were
other Trolls who loved different kinds of music.

There were Rocker Trolls, Classical Trolls, Country Western Trolls, Funk Trolls and Techno Trolls. King Peppy opened a map showing where each of the six Trolls tribes lived.

Every tribe had a special string to make their music.
'I get it!' Poppy said. 'Queen Barb wants to bring
the six strings together so we can make music for a big,
happy party!'

Branch and King Peppy weren't so sure. They
thought Queen Barb was planning to TAKE their string!
'You can't trust other Trolls,' King Peppy warned.
'They're different from us!'

But differences didn't matter to Poppy.
They were all Trolls!

Poppy left to meet the other Trolls in a balloon called Sheila B. and Branch went along to help Poppy and keep her safe. Biggie and Mr Dinkles also went, by accident. They'd climbed into the balloon to eat the cotton candy Poppy had for Barb and they'd fallen asleep.

'Time for a Trolls World Tour!' Poppy exclaimed.

The first land they reached was Symphonyville,
where the Classical Trolls lived – but it had been
destroyed! A little flute named Pennywhistle explained
that Queen Barb had used loud rock music to blast the
town and steal their string!

Poppy realised they had to stop
Queen Barb. But they'd need
help from the other Trolls...

Soon Poppy, Branch, Biggie and Mr Dinkles arrived
in Lonesome Flats, where Mayor Delta Dawn and
the other Country Western Trolls lived. Their music
sounded sad, so Poppy decided to cheer them
up with a rad medley of pop tunes.

The Country Western Trolls DISLIKED the pop music!
They threw Poppy and the others in a jail cell.
'I only wanted to unite the Trolls,' Poppy said.

Luckily, a Country Western Troll named Hickory
helped them escape. 'I love your message about music
bringing Trolls together,' he explained.

The Country Western Trolls chased Hickory and the Pop Trolls right off a cliff and

into

a river!

SPLASH!

Hickory built a fancy raft to carry them
to safety.
'Funk Trolls, here we come!' Poppy cried.

Far down the river, the Pop Trolls spotted a giant spaceship in the sky! Poppy checked her map and saw a drawing of a spaceship that looked just like the one overhead.

'I think we've found the Funk Trolls!' Poppy
announced.

Suddenly, beams of light shone on the Pop Trolls
and drew them up into the ship!

Poppy was honoured to meet the King and
Queen of Funk – and to see her friend Cooper! He
had discovered that his Trolls tribe was the Funk Trolls.

Suddenly, Queen Barb and her army
of Rocker Trolls attacked!
'We're here for your string, Funk Trolls!'
the queen snarled. 'Hand it over!'

Thinking quickly, Cooper protected his friends
by ejecting them from the ship in a bubble.
Branch was ready to head back to Trolls Village
so they could protect the pop string, but Poppy
pulled it out of her hair.

'It's right here!' she said.

When Queen Barb saw the pop music string, she
zoomed down and snatched it out of Poppy's hand!
Then she ordered her Rocker Trolls to grab Poppy
and take her to Volcano Rock City for the big concert!

'Now that I have all the strings,' Queen Barb boasted, 'I'm going to play the ultimate power chord! It'll turn ALL Trolls into ROCKER TROLLS!'

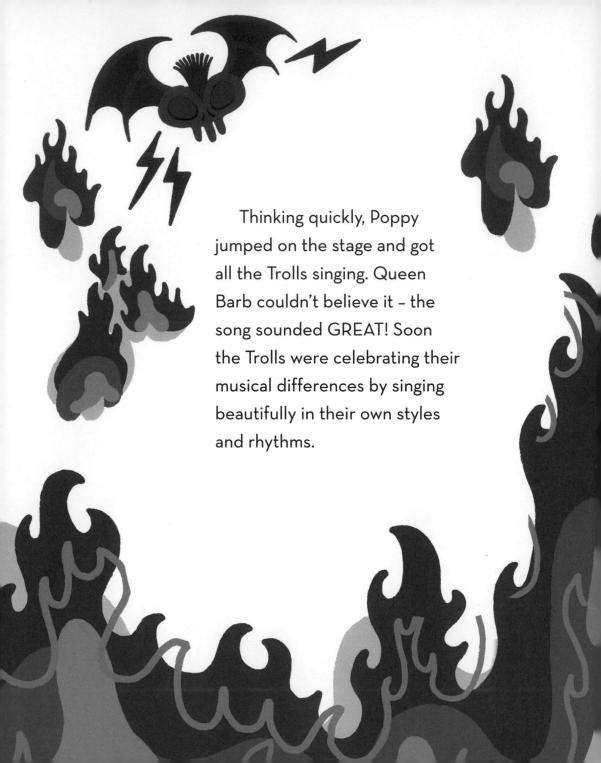

Thinking quickly, Poppy
jumped on the stage and got
all the Trolls singing. Queen
Barb couldn't believe it – the
song sounded GREAT! Soon
the Trolls were celebrating their
musical differences by singing
beautifully in their own styles
and rhythms.

IT WAS A GREAT SONG!

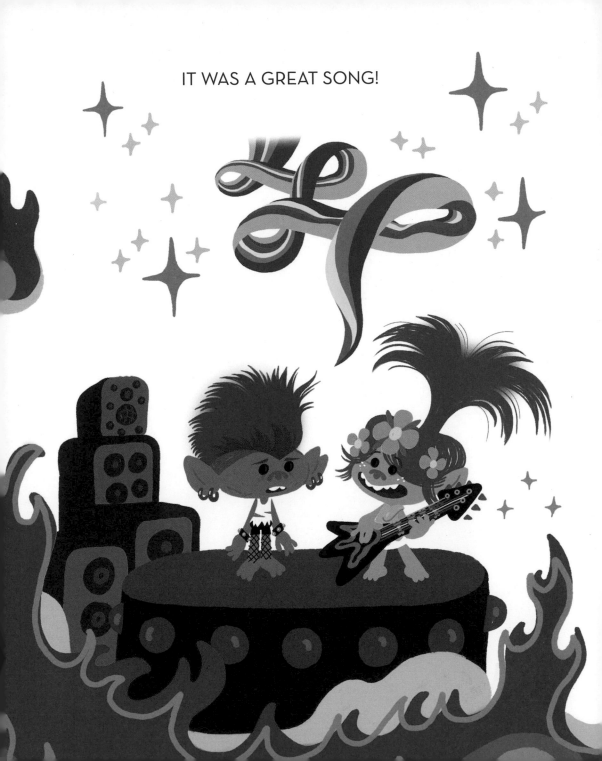

The Trolls sang and danced together.
They were different from one another, but
they *ALL* LOVED MUSIC!

The Trolls made happy music well into the night. From then on, everyone lived in perfect harmony!

Treasure Cove Stories

Please contact Centum Books to receive the full list of titles in the *Treasure Cove Stories* series.
books@centumbooksltd.co.uk

Classic favourites

1 Three Little Pigs
2 Snow White and the Seven Dwarfs
3 The Fox and the Hound
- Hide-and-Seek
4 Dumbo
5 Cinderella
6 Cinderella's Friends
7 Alice in Wonderland
8 Mad Hatter's Tea Party from Alice in Wonderland
9 Mickey Mouse and his Spaceship
10 Peter Pan
11 Pinocchio
12 Mickey and the Beanstalk
13 Sleeping Beauty and the Good Fairies
14 The Lucky Puppy
15 Chicken Little
16 The Incredibles
17 Coco
18 Winnie the Pooh and Tigger
19 The Sword in the Stone
20 Mary Poppins
21 The Jungle Book
22 The Aristocats
23 Lady and the Tramp
24 Bambi
25 Bambi - Friends of the Forest

Recently published

50 Frozen
51 Cinderella is my Babysitter
52 Beauty and the Beast
- I am the Beast
53 Blaze and the Monster Machines
- Mighty Monster Machines
54 Blaze and the Monster Machines
- Dino Parade!
55 Teenage Mutant Ninja Turtles
- Follow the Ninja!

56 I am a Princess
57 The Big Book of Paw Patrol
58 Paw Patrol
- Adventures with Grandpa!
59 Paw Patrol - Pirate Pups!
60 Trolls
61 Trolls Holiday
62 The Secret Life of Pets
63 Zootropolis
64 Ariel is my Babysitter
65 Tiana is my Babysitter
66 Belle is my Babysitter
67 Paw Patrol
- Itty-Bitty Kitty Rescue
68 Moana
69 Nella the Princess Knight
- My Heart is Bright!
70 Guardians of the Galaxy
71 Captain America
- High-Stakes Heist!
72 Ant-Man
73 The Mighty Avengers
74 The Mighty Avengers
- Lights Out!
75 The Incredible Hulk
76 Shimmer & Shine
- Wish Upon a Sleepover
77 Shimmer & Shine - Backyard Ballet
78 Paw Patrol - All-Star Pups!
79 Teenage Mutant Ninja Turtles
- Really Spaced Out!
80 I am Ariel
81 Madagascar
82 Jasmine is my Babysitter
83 How to Train your Dragon
84 Shrek
85 Puss in Boots
86 Kung Fu Panda
87 Beauty and the Beast - I am Belle
88 The Lion Guard
- The Imaginary Okapi
89 Thor - Thunder Strike!
90 Guardians of the Galaxy
- Rocket to the Rescue!
91 Nella the Princess Knight
- Nella and the Dragon
92 Shimmer & Shine
- Treasure Twins!

93 Olaf's Frozen Adventure
94 Black Panther
95 Trolls
- Branch's Bunker Birthday
96 Trolls - Poppy's Party
97 The Ugly Duckling
98 Cars - Look Out for Mater!
99 101 Dalmatians
100 The Sorcerer's Apprentice
101 Tangled
102 Avengers
- The Threat of Thanos
103 Puppy Dog Pals
- Don't Rain on my Pug-Rade
104 Jurassic Park
105 The Mighty Thor
106 Doctor Strange

Latest publications

107 Captain Marvel
108 The Invincible Iron Man
109 Black Panther
- Warriors of Wakanda
110 The Big Freeze
111 Ratatouille
112 Aladdin
113 Aladdin - I am the Genie
114 Seven Dwarfs Find a House
115 Toy Story
116 Toy Story 4
117 Paw Patrol - Jurassic Bark!
118 Paw Patrol
- Mighty Pup Power!
119 Shimmer & Shine
- Pet Talent Show!
120 SpongeBob SquarePants
- Krabby Patty Caper
121 The Lion King - I am Simba
122 Winnie the Pooh
- The Honey Tree
123 Frozen II
124 Baby Shark and the Colours of the Ocean
125 Baby Shark and the Police Sharks!
126 Trolls World Tour

Book list may be subject to change.